HOW NOT TO BECOME AN INFLUENCER

KATHRYN REIGN

How NOT to Become an Influencer

Cover Design by Lara Wynter (Wynter Designs)

CONTENTS

HOW **NOT** TO BECOME AN INFLUENCER

KATHRYN REIGN

*N*ikki met the guy at a bar last Friday night when she was out with her friends. *His name?* Not important. She could have any man she wanted, and since he was too self-absorbed to not call her again, HE didn't deserve a name.

Anyhow, Nikki had agreed to go on a date with him. At an Italian restaurant, of course. Nikki deserved only the best. And, as usual, she couldn't stop talking. But why would she? She had far more interesting things to say than anyone else, and so she talked and talked.

"As I was saying, I'm just so lucky to be this successful at my job. I see all these people struggling to find their calling in life and, to me, it came so easi-ly," she said, leaning forward and invading the guy's personal space a little too much for a girl he'd only known for fifteen minutes.

"And… What is it that you do? Something in marketing, right?" he asked, leaning back against his chair.

"That's what I majored in, yeah. But I find it boring. My job is much better than that," she exclaimed, twirling one of her curls around her finger and lifting her chin.

"So, what do you do?" he asked again, raising his eyebrows with an obvious annoyance.

"I'm a fashion influencer!" she sang with confidence and pride.

He just stared at her, and then let out a cackle.

"I'm sorry, but that's not a job. That's girls playing dress-up for an audience."

Red blotches appeared on Nikki's face and neck like spring flowers.

"So typical," she huffed. "You millennials think you have to bust your ass to earn money, or it doesn't count. That's so pathetic."

An awkward silence followed. Diffusing the tension in the air a little, the waiter picked the perfect moment to come over and ask for their order.

"What can I get you?" he asked with enthusiasm, smiling widely.

"A cosmopolitan for me," said Nikki, mirroring the same enthusiasm as though she didn't just offend her date a second ago.

"One cosmopolitan coming right up. And for you, sir?" the waiter asked.

"Just a coke, please," he said with uneasiness.

"Oh, come on! Live a little!" Nikki made a mocking expression to the waiter, as if her date was being too uptight.

"The coke is fine," he said to the waiter again, motioning for him to go fetch the drinks.

Becoming focused, Nikki stared at her phone for a good five minutes while her date looked around the room, utterly bored. Suddenly, the silence was broken by a high-pitched scream.

"I can't believe it! They responded to my message!" Nikki squealed with a dreamy expression on her face, eyes wide with both excitement and surprise.

Her date cleared his throat, as if reminding her that he was still there. Or maybe uncomfortable about her outbreak. "Who did? What message?"

"My favorite brand! They want me to post a photo with one of their dresses! What a fantastic evening! I'm drinking my favorite drink, inside my favorite restaurant, and… and now this!" Her eyes were shining with true emotion, and Nikki let out a delightful cry.

The date looked at her, appalled, while she continued to type on her phone.

"Just out of curiosity, how much do they pay for something like that?" he asked after a while.

She didn't respond, still typing. And then, "Huh?" Nikki shot her head up, finally pulling her attention away from her phone. "What was that?"

"I said, how much do they pay you to post a picture on your profile?"

Nikki straightened her back and lifted her chin even higher. "Well, I'm still at the beginning of my career. They just give me free products and services for now. This dress I'm supposed to post a picture in? I get to keep it, you know?"

"Oh," he replied.

Nikki thought he looked embarrassed, and she shot him an annoyed glance before she continued typing on her phone, replying to the brand before she lost the great opportunity.

The waiter soon brought the drinks over.

"And have you decided on your dinner for tonight?" he asked as he placed the drinks on the table.

Just as Nikki opened her mouth, her date interrupted her. "You know what? I'm not hungry. I had a big lunch, and I just got a text that I have to get back to work."

"On a Saturday?" asked Nikki with that high-pitched voice she only used when she was truly shocked.

"Yes," he answered.

The waiter stood awkwardly by the table in obvious discomfort while Nikki crossed her arms over her chest.

"Okay, then," Nikki replied, shaking her head slightly as if to shake off the acceptance of the abrupt end to her date.

"Before I leave, a toast to your new gig!" Her date lifted the coke to her, as if offering an apology for his bad timing.

"Wait, don't drink yet!" Nikki exclaimed and reached down to grab her phone.

"Why?" he asked, looking puzzled.

"I have to record this, for social media! It's very important for my brand that I post regularly and show what I'm up to."

Her date looked around, uncomfortable, and he meekly clinked his coke with her drink as Nikki recorded.

"Oh, wait, it wasn't recording! Let's do it again. And could you look happier this time?"

"Why, sure." There were no emotions in his words, but Nikki didn't care; she simply recorded again.

The man drank his drink in silence as Nikki became lost in her own little world of social media, adding filters and tags to her story. After a while, she finally lifted her head, only to see that her date had already finished his drink. The ice in her untouched cosmopolitan had melted, so she drank it in one gulp.

"So, which club for tonight? I'm thinking… Phantom?" she asked, batting her lashes at him.

"I already told you, I have to work," he said. "I finished my drink to be polite, but I have to be on my way now."

"I thought that was just an excuse so you wouldn't have to pay for dinner."

He looked at her, stunned, and then he smiled, getting up slowly.

"Okay, let's go."

In a bit of a rush, he went to the counter and paid the bill while Nikki kept scrolling on her phone, liking and commenting on as many posts as she could.

Once at the front of the restaurant, they stood in an awkward silence. Actually, he did; Nikki was carefully putting on lip gloss, admiring herself in her pocket mirror, completely oblivious to the guy's uneasiness.

"Well, goodbye, Nikki," he said finally.

"Such a shame you have to leave. What did you say you do for a living again?"

"I didn't say. I'm an emergency physician. A colleague isn't feeling well, so I'm going in to finish his shift tonight."

Nikki's eyes suddenly showed interest… for the first time that entire night.

"Wow. You must earn a lot of money, then," she said shamelessly.

"Uhm… Alright, I have to go now. You have a

good night." He waved awkwardly, and then quickly rushed to the parking lot.

"Wait! Aren't you going to drive me home?" Nikki yelled after him, her heels clicking on the gravel.

A couple of people smoking in front of the restaurant chuckled, their eyes on the awkward couple.

When he didn't reply and simply jumped in his car and left, Nikki shoved her hair back and smiled. "How rude of him, right?" she said to none of them in particular, still smiling and not understanding that they were laughing at her, not with her.

Nikki stood in front of the restaurant for ten more minutes, filming yet another video with a new glass of cosmopolitan before writing a catchy caption: *A well-deserved drink and a hot date. Could my Saturday get any better?*

She posted it and beamed with satisfaction before proceeding to take a selfie. Her makeup was flawless. Of course, that wouldn't have mattered anyway as Nikki was lucky enough to have been born with natural beauty. Some people were just born lucky.

Waiting for a cab, Nikki tentatively counted the number of views on her story. Fifty so far. Saturdays were important for influencers, as a lot of lonely people with nowhere to go would be checking their phones, admiring her lifestyle.

"How was the restaurant last night? Was it packed?" Nikki's friend, Demi, asked her the next day as they talked on the phone.

"I feel so hungover right now. He kept buying me cosmopolitans, trying to get me drunk!" Nikki laughed, leaning back on her desk chair and admiring the manicured nails on her free hand.

There were stacks of magazines on her desk, and papers of things she had meant to do, but she'd get to it once she was done with the call. Maybe. For someone who loved fashion as much as Nikki did, who had asked their parents for a sewing machine for Christmas ten years straight, it would seem that working at a fashion design company was the perfect job.

But it wasn't. Having deadlines, a passive aggressive boss whom she was convinced didn't do anything at all except look menacing at her desk, and a tiny office wasn't her thing. Nikki hated desk duty, and her boss even more.

"What was he like?" Demi asked. "He looked so hot in the pictures and videos you posted! You're so lucky!" Demi was always very enthusiastic. She had been Nikki's best, and often, only friend, and they'd known each other for years.

"Well, he was very serious. And guess what he does?"

"What?"

"He's a doctor! He works in the ER! We actually had to cut the date short before he could get me drunk and back to his place because they called him in for an emergency shift."

Nikki smiled, even though there was no one there to see her, but she had to believe everything she was saying. It was the key to being who she was, to becoming a famous fashion influencer.

If she didn't act with her inner circle the same way she did online, then what's the point? She had to be who she wanted to be *all the time*!

Her boss walked past her office cubicle then, talking with an intern, and she shot her a nasty look before disappearing from view.

"On a Saturday?" Demi was asking. "That's so annoying that he ruined your night."

"I know, right? " Nikki replied, completely ignoring her boss' warning look. "When you ask a girl out on a date, you should at least drive her home safely! But you know these doctor types, they get lost in their work and can't seem to leave the work at work. Their personal lives are shit."

"I'm sure he'll feel bad for leaving so abruptly and ask you out again tonight," Demi reassured her, her tone soft and caring.

"Of course, he will," said Nikki. "We should also hang out soon. You haven't posted any outings over the weekend."

"Oh, it's fine. I was mostly at home." Demi sounded unconcerned, which made Nikki more nervous.

"Demi, this is why you only have a couple

hundred followers, because you don't put in the effort! You need to post more often."

"Well, I don't want more followers. I only follow people I know personally."

"Do you really want to work at a bank your entire life? Wear the same boring clothes, live paycheck to paycheck?"

There was a short pause on the line, and then, "What's wrong with that?"

"It's just so boring!" Nikki groaned.

At that moment, her boss stomped inside, not caring to close the door behind her. As Nikki suspected, the usual ugly breath was escaping her mouth at a disturbing rate. Nikki had to completely freeze her body to avoid cringing at the sight.

"Nikki, you were ten minutes late today. And now I find you on the phone. Again." Her body shook as she spoke, and she looked as though she would collapse at any moment.

Taking a deep breath, Nikki spoke into her phone. "Sorry, Demi, gotta go. Catch up later."

"Good luck," whispered Demi. "Just be nice to the witch, and it'll be fine."

Nikki hung up as her boss looked at her with her arms crossed over her chest, and an angry scowl on her face.

"I'm so sorry," she said simply, shrugging a little. "It won't happen again." Nikki didn't bother with excuses. Not only did she not care about giving the woman an explanation, but she also had a feeling that she wouldn't take it.

"I'd forgive you if you hadn't been late yesterday also, or the morning before."

The words dripped through her teeth, and Nikki knew that she was in big trouble. Even though her brain was very well aware that she was on the cusp of losing her job, her heart hadn't sped up at all. Her breathing was regular, her pulse rate was regular, and her mind was clear. Nikki realized then just how much she disliked that job.

"Follow me into my office," the woman told Nikki. She turned around and exited first, followed by Nikki, and then they walked toward the dragon's den.

Her boss, whose name Nikki didn't care about either, had golden brown hair, freshly curled and healthy. Her face was caked in makeup, and her clothes were always expensive and colorful, usually in pastel colors. From a single glance, she would seem like a very nice woman, one who took care of herself and was extremely professional.

To be honest, that had been Nikki's first impression of her, too. But deep down, she was a dragon trying to hide all the riches from the rest of the world, to have everything for herself.

"Nikki, I'm sure you understand why you're here, so I won't go into details. Normally, if your absences had been more spread out, I may have been able to overlook them. Or if I didn't find you playing at your desk instead of working mostly every day. However, this seems to be a recurring incident, your lateness and lack of attention. Lack of dedication." There was a short pause, one laced with bad news. "I'm sorry, Nikki, but I have to let you go." The corners of her mouth were twitching as she forced back a grin.

Good riddance to you, too.

"I understand," Nikki replied curtly. "I'll pack up my things." If there was one thing she didn't intend to show, it was that she cared.

A weird sigh of relief escaped Nikki's mouth as she strolled away from Hell with a box tucked under her arm. That had been her only job and way of supporting herself at the moment, but anything would be better than that place.

After all, her life as an influencer was growing by the day, and soon, she wouldn't even need a day job.

BACK AT HOME, Nikki made herself the third cup of coffee that day and lit up a cigarette. Her one-week-long success in giving up cigarettes proved to be… stupid. Cigarettes were a part of her image. You know, Italian femme. Every girl-boss smoked, and she wasn't going to be the exception.

Checking her phone, she was once again disappointed to see that her date hadn't messaged her.

Could he still be at work?

Nikki had heard that doctors sometimes worked

twenty-four-hour long shifts. She could never do that. Her own time was too valuable.

Deciding that he was definitely still at work, she started working on herself.

Shoot for the stars, Nikki. Shoot for the stars, she thought.

CHAPTER 2

*N*ikki had gotten herself lost and was sure she looked like an idiot or a tourist. Trying not to blame herself for it and to calm down, she grabbed her phone and scrolled for a bit. She even posted a selfie with the caption: *Losing myself in the big city!*

She hadn't lived in New York City her whole life, and there were still parts where she hadn't explored.

Plus, the city was so big that even the rats got lost at times.

After what seemed like an eternity of wandering around, Nikki happened to walk past a school with a big banner that caught her attention. It was hanging up on the front of the building, a big and white colored sheet with dandelion yellow writing that said: *Prom Night, May 15th. Luxury for all.*

Gosh! Nikki remembered her prom. It definitely hadn't been the fairy tale she thought it would be, but she didn't want to even think about it.

There were several kids walking around, and most of them looked like they were seniors in high school. Nikki wondered what they would wear to their prom, and mentally, she pictured the perfect dress for the two girls walking closest to her.

The perfect color, fabric, waistline. It'd been a long time since Nikki had used her sewing machine, as she preferred to buy her clothes from known brands than wear her own. But once, when she was younger, it had been her greatest hobby and aspiration. To be a fashion designer.

But no, she wasn't good enough, and her looks were better than her sewing, so she decided to stick to fashion modeling and influencing instead.

But a prom… Having no job meant no money that month, which meant she had to find a way to pay her rent. If she could make dresses for these girls and charge half of it as advance payments, then she'd have enough to pay this month's rent, and the next.

By then, she should be able to afford her life as an influencer, right?

The idea of starting her own business had occurred to her multiple times throughout her life. Nikki knew she had the intelligence for it, and her father would've lent her the money to start. However, she doubted her skills.

But these girls needed a prom dress, not something for a high fashion runway, so she knew she could deliver.

Nikki tried to not think about her own prom fiasco as she walked back home. Her dress, the one she made herself, had gotten caught on a nail while walking into school and ripped—ending in her running away from prom.

This time, it would be different.

She would make the perfect dresses for these girls, and neither of them would tear. The idea of making those frilly things for a living sent a shiver down her spine for a hot second, but Nikki kept her emotions in check.

It was just a quick job to survive the month. She would thrive as an influencer; that was her calling. Making dresses was just a silly hobby, something she'd do again just to get by for a little while. Just until her career as an influencer peaked, and she could make a living out of that.

Flyers would get the word out, Nikki thought when she was back at home, finding pictures of her old designs and working a little magic on one of her editing apps. Whether or not the word would spread was a different story, but she was confident that it would work.

That day, Nikki worked for hours making sure her flyers were perfect, while in between, she kept posting on social media—a few selfies and coffee pictures—and also sent about twenty applications to different brands so she could promote them.

The next morning, she returned to the school with the prom banner.

"Excuse me," she said as she approached some of the girls outside, sounding like she owned the world. "I'm a fashion designer," she added, handing them each a flyer with pictures of some of her previous work. "I was walking past and couldn't help but notice the banner on the front of the building, the one about your prom. I was wondering, do you need someone to design and make your prom dresses for you?"

Nikki tried to keep her chin high and not feel embarrassed to resort to designing for children, but she told herself it was fine. It would only be for a short while.

"None of us have been able to get one so far," the girl closest to her replied. "We've been shopping around for quite a while now, but every time we find a dress we like and look at the price tag, it goes way beyond our budget."

"That's perfect! Believe me, I won't disappoint."

She talked to the girls for a little longer, making sure she explained how the dresses would have to be paid, half in advance and half on the day she delivered them, and then she started walking home.

Back at home, there was a closet full of fabrics that would finally be able to fulfill their use, and Nikki would get to use her sewing machine once again. When she first started working at Hell, she had lost all motivation to design and sew. Being surrounded by fashion design all day, and then coming home to do more fashion design was too much.

Which was why Nikki had started working on her influencer career… Most days, by the time she got home, she refused to even look at her sewing machine. But without the office job now, it would be different. It had to.

That's exactly the reason why they tell you not to make a job out of a hobby—it ruins the hobby and transforms it into a chore.

Getting off the elevator and walking to her apartment door, Nikki was excited to see that a package had been left on her doorstep.

Things were just getting better and better!

CHAPTER 3

It was the dress that her sponsors had sent her. Overjoyed, Nikki entered her apartment and ripped the package open like a Christmas gift, only to find it so… ugly.

Why would they send her this one? This wasn't her style, not at all. Nikki assumed that they'd at least check her feed first so they could pick something that was appropriate to her style.

Oh, well. That's business.

Along with the package came a note:

Dearest Nikky,

We are so glad you offered to promote one of our dresses. Please take a picture with it, and post it on your profile and stories. Please don't get the dress dirty or wrinkled.

Nikki was annoyed with them spelling her name wrong, and then confused as to why it mattered if the dress got wrinkled, as it was hers to keep anyway. Confused, she kept on reading.

Since your following is less than a thousand, we consider this partnership to benefit you more than it benefits us. However, we decided to give you a chance. Because of this, we ask that you send the package to the address that's at the bottom of this note, so the next influencer can promote it, too.

Once again, thank you for the collaboration. And we hope you shop with us soon.

Her heart started racing. Did they know who she was? Sure, she had eight hundred and fifty-seven followers now, but anyone with experience in this line of work knew that it's the rate of increase that counts. Nikki was up thirty-four followers just this week! Followers had been going up and down, but that also happened often, so she wasn't concerned about it.

And the audacity to spell her name with a "Y!"

If she were to succeed, she needed to develop a thicker skin.

That's business.

So, Nikki got up and tidied her one-bedroom apartment to get a better background.

Then she took the hideous dress out of the box and carefully put it on.

It was green. Not a classy, seaweed green. It was lime green. Who was she? The Grinch? And worse, it was too big on her, making her look like a green sack of potatoes. Or a zucchini.

Unsure of what to do next, Nikki looked around the apartment, only to find her sewing machine on top of the table, staring at her.

That's it! She would fix the dress, make it a little smaller, and then she'd take the stitching out before sending it to the next influencer. The brand would never know, and her pictures would look much better.

Stripping down to her underwear, she sat on the table and got to work. The dress was meant to fit her like a globe, so she made some adjustments to the sides, and then on the back. Problem was, how to put it on, as she had sewn over the zip on the back, and the fabric didn't stretch at all. Taking those stitches out, Nikki decided to put the dress on before finishing the alterations. That way, it would fit her just perfectly.

She wiggled the dress on, grabbed a needle, and made some stitches on the back with the dress put on backwards. Then she wiggled a little more until the dress was the right way around. It wasn't an easy feat, and Nikki was a little sweaty by the time it was all over.

Still, like a professional, she put on some makeup, found some nice matching jewelry, and put on her best smile. Then, placing her phone on her tripod, she moved around in different poses, gazing into the distance, blowing a kiss, winking. And through it all, making sure the stitches wouldn't be seen on camera.

After an hour, she was satisfied with her work.

She picked the best photo and got to editing, using her favorite app without even taking the dress off. It'd be hard to, and she wanted to get the posting over with first. Of course, she had to make her nose smaller and smooth out her face. The bags under her eyes had to go, too. A few inches off her waist, and a few to her chest. A dramatic filter, and her job was done.

"A perfect outfit doesn't exist… oh, wait."

Feeling sexy, Nikki decided to message the cute doctor who took her out the night before. She sent him the photo she just took.

"Thinking of you!" she said as she typed.

His green circle was lit. He was online.

Seen, it said underneath her photo, and Nikki waited for his reply. But it didn't seem to come.

He was probably still at work.

Trying to forget all about it, Nikki went to take the dress off. But when she moved her hands to her back, trying to spin the dress around to undo the stitches…

The dress ripped.

She panicked when she heard the sound of ripping fabric. She wiggled around, trying to get the dress off, but the more she moved, the more the fabric ripped. Taking the dress off was the only thing on her mind at that moment; she had to fix the tear somehow.

She attempted to remove an arm, but the dress was so stiff and tight that it was almost physically impossible to move. She tried again, but still nothing.

The panic continued for about an hour before Nikki's arms grew so weak and tired that she gave up entirely. Getting stuck in a dress was such a stupid thing for a twenty-five-year-old adult to do that she couldn't help but laugh. Laughter that was also mixed with frustration and tears of rage.

What could she do? She couldn't get it off and could barely breathe. Her head was racing, having a complete breakdown. Whatever she did, she couldn't stay inside any longer. Nikki almost felt like her eighteen-year-old self again as she rushed out of the apartment, tears still lingering in her eyes as she ran away.

She ran with a ripped dress. Only this time, she didn't know how to get out of it.

Running to the end of the hall, Nikki knocked on the door of the cute old lady who lived there. She waited for a minute, and when the door didn't open, she knocked again.

"Ms. Patterson! It's me, Nikki with an I! I need your help!"

She knocked and knocked, but no one came. Growing desperate by the minute, Nikki went to the elevator. She didn't know many of the neighbors, but there was a guy on the fifth floor whom she had hooked up with once. Maybe he could give her a hand.

But just her luck, when she jumped into the elevator, it started moving as soon as she closed the door… before she could choose the floor. And it was going up! And up. And up.

The moment the door opened up in the Penthouse, Nikki's jaw dropped.

They say people often meet the love of their life when they least expect it. Nikki always thought it meant that she wouldn't have any makeup on, and she would be in her sweatpants. And maybe that's why she made sure to never wear sweatpants in public, or go out without at least mascara and lipstick on. If she were to meet the love of her life when she least expected it, she wasn't going to take any chances.

You can only leave one first impression, after all.

The day Nikki met Prince Charming wasn't an ordinary day. She was wearing a torn dress, and tears were still wet on her cheeks. And Prince Charming was at the door of the elevator, staring right into her eyes.

"Are you okay? Are you lost?" the man asked.

His voice was smooth, and there were no cracks. His hair was a hazelnut brown, and it lengthened to his nape at the back; at the front, it was parted in the middle and particularly wavy. He was dressed in a white shirt and black jeans, and he looked very well taken care of, his skin clear, soft lips, and an upturned nose.

Look at me. I'm having a panic attack while stuck in a dress, but I have no trouble studying a pretty man's face. And a rich one at that if this man lives in a penthouse.

He must've been over six feet tall, and he had a dashing smile and piercing blue eyes. Most importantly, he was impeccably dressed. A black polo shirt, dark blue jeans, and the latest branded sneakers, all pulled together with a stylish pair of sunglasses. The man knew how to dress.

"Worse, I'm stuck," Nikki mumbled in a strangled voice.

"What was that?" the man asked, holding the door of the elevator so it wouldn't close on her.

"I'm Nikki," she said a little louder, using her most dashing smile right back at him and forgetting a little bit about the drama she was stuck in.

"Nice to meet you, Nikki. I'm Scotty. This is not the way I like to meet girls as beautiful as you, by almost crashing into them." He chuckled without a trace of shyness on his face. "I do like it when they come visit me, though, but I don't think you meant to come up here."

Nikki giggled, already picturing their wedding. Was she a fall bride or a summer one? Should they have a big wedding or a small one? How many brides-maids? How excited would Demi be to be her maid of honor?

"Anyhow, I was just about to go down and grab a coffee," Scotty continued. "Would you like to join me?" he asked, interrupting her daydream, yet confirming the validity of her fantasy.

"That sounds great! But first, I need help getting out of this dress," Nikki replied. "I'm stuck," she admitted, showing the rip on the side and the stitches.

"I assume you don't have any spare clothes on you?"

"No, sorry... I could go down to my apartment and fetch some."

"No worries, do you mind borrowing some of mine? I'll get you a shirt, and I think I have an old pair of sweats that will fit just fine."

"Thank you so much." Nikki was dreadfully self-conscious, in a stranger's home and about to wear his clothes, clothes that would probably not fit her the way she liked. But she couldn't pass up the perfect occasion to meet this guy and know more about him.

What if she went to get changed in her own apart-ment, and the guy left or something? She couldn't risk it. She had found her rich Prince Charming, and she'd do whatever was needed to *wow* him.

A few minutes went by, and Scotty returned with a blue shirt that looked to be about two sizes too big, as well as a pair of black sweats.

"I can help you cut the dress; it looks like it's already ripped, anyway." Nikki paled, and Scotty might have thought she was embarrassed or some-thing. "Don't worry, I won't look." Nikki thought she'd actually prefer if Scotty were paying attention while he had sharp scissors close to her body. But she didn't say so.

She also wished she could save the dress, but she wasn't sure if that would be possible anymore. She felt hideously uneasy letting a stranger help her with such a thing, but she had no choice, unfortunately. And maybe Scotty would like the little skin he'd get to see.

Scotty started cutting at the dress through the stitches that Nikki had made. She let him watch, and she held the fabric close to her body as he did so. Her heart felt heavy. She had spent so much time getting the brand to accept her proposal, and now it was being cut up, probably ruined. She'd have to use her savings to buy the same dress to send to the next person.

When Scotty finished cutting and turned around, Nikki let the dress fall to the floor and put on the shirt, tying it with a knot at the front so it wouldn't look hideous. She also rolled the sleeves three quarters up, and left the first two buttons undone. There was not much to do about the sweatpants, but they didn't look half as bad as she expected; they were only slightly baggy.

"I'm ready," Nikki said, and Scotty turned back around, smiling widely when he saw her. "Thanks, Scotty," she added, realizing that she was saying his name for the first time.

I better remember this moment. The day I met the man of my dreams. Our grandkids will definitely ask about it.

"Looks better on you than me," Scotty teased. "I guess I'm gonna have to let you keep it."

"Oh, no, it's okay. I'll return it tomorrow! Washed and all."

"It's okay. Really, you can keep it. I don't live here; this is my parents' place in the city. I was just passing through to get some things."

"Well…" Nikki bit her lip and battered her lashes, knowing that she was more than able to wow this guy. "Maybe we can exchange numbers, and I can run it to your place when it's clean."

Scotty smiled, pointing back to the elevator.

"Why don't we exchange numbers over coffee? I was about to go out for one."

"Sounds like a perfect plan," Nikki replied, picking up the dress from the floor and folding it under her arm.

She'd deal with that mess after her first date with her future husband.

CHAPTER 4

The day of Nikki's wedding, she expected tears of joy. She expected happiness and plenty of smiles. But the reality was far from her imagination.

"Demi, where the fuck are my cigarettes? You expect me to go through the entire day without nicotine? Are you out of your mind?" Nikki screamed at her friend in front of everyone. The other bridesmaids looked at each other awkwardly. The street traffic outside the window suddenly became very interesting to the photographer.

"You told me you didn't want to have cigarette breath on your wedding day, Nikki," Demi answered patiently, as though speaking to a small child.

"You should've known me better than that. After all, aren't you my maid of honor? Your duty is to keep me happy!" Nikki stared at Demi with anger, red blotches appearing on her face despite the heavy foundation.

Demi made the mistake of following the trail of blotches with her eyes. Nikki turned to the mirror and looked at herself.

"I can't believe this is happening! You're making me look terrible! You know I always turn red when I'm upset! Get me my cigarettes, NOW!" Nikki screamed at her.

Her mother peeked in through the door to see what the fuss was about, but Nikki shot her a look that said, "You better not," and her mother quickly disappeared. Nobody wanted to stand in the middle of the bridal warzone in case they got verbally shot.

Demi was about to leave to go to the nearest store to buy Nikki her cigarettes when she pointed at her, glaring.

"Where are you going?" Nikki asked.

The photographer rolled his eyes behind Nikki's back, and Demi looked terrified for a hot second.

"To… get you your cigarettes, Nikki," Demi answered.

"Are you insane? We're in the middle of the photoshoot! Just tell your boyfriend to get them!" Nikki threw back with a dismissive tone.

Demi left, and Nikki turned to the photographer.

"So! Let's start posing, shall we? Lori! Take my phone, and record as many videos as you can. I need this blasted all over social media!"

"Don't worry, darling. I'll take plenty of photos and videos for you," the photographer assured her.

"And when will they be available?" Nikki asked impatiently.

"With editing, it would take… I guess about two weeks?" Lori replied innocently.

"That's exactly my point. I don't mean to be a nag, but I *am* an influencer. I don't expect you to know what that is, so I'll explain it to you. I'm a brand, a social media presence. Hundreds of people follow me and can't wait to see how I look in my wedding dress. Do you really think they'll wait two weeks? I've been building up to this moment for a month!"

The photographer looked at her with a blank expression, not understanding a word she had just said.

"Oh, come on! If you're going to be this slow, I can just set your camera on a timer and do the job myself! Do I need to do that? Do you want to lose your job?" she continued to scream at her.

The poor woman rushed to her position at the back of the room, terrified of getting her head ripped off.

"Come on, girls! I want a couple of shots with you and the… lovely bride," she hesitated.

The bridesmaids gathered carefully around Nikki and posed, no one saying a single word.

After what seemed like an eternity, the photoshoot was over. Demi had returned with the cigarettes, and Nikki grabbed them eagerly from her hands. She went outside, dragging her giant puffy dress alongside herself.

Like a person who'd been starving for a long, long time, Nikki took a greedy puff of the cig.

"The groom is here!" announced Demi cheerfully a moment later, but Nikki didn't hear her from the balcony.

Excited, Scotty entered the room with the biggest smile on his face. At that moment, Nikki was coming back inside. At the sight of his bride, Scotty's entire face lit up. In comparison, Nikki's was the epitome of terror.

"Hi, my love… You look…" Scotty was then interrupted by a scared shriek.

"What are you doing here?! Who let you in? The first time you see me is supposed to be documented by the photographer!!! I've told you that a thousand times, Scotty! Now my one chance to get one of those photos of the groom seeing his bride for the first time is ruined!" Nikki started crying before she was done talking, and she ran out of the room past him, locking herself in the bathroom.

Stunned, Scotty looked after her, not realizing what a big deal that photo was to Nikki. Nobody did.

"Please, Nikki… babe, come out of the bathroom!" Scotty pleaded on the other side of the door a few minutes later, something that had been going on for a while. "I know how badly you wanted that photo, and I apologize from the bottom of my heart. We can still do the photo! I'll just forget I already saw you, and I'll try to put on my best surprised face. I'll even shed a tear of joy. Please, just come out."

Scotty had spoken the magic words. The door unlocked, and a smiling Nikki walked out.

"For real? Can we take the picture, Scotty?"

"Of course, my love," whispered Scotty with a forced smile.

A shared sigh was heard in the room; everyone was relieved that Nikki had come out. The photographer rushed to get to them before Nikki could yell at her again.

"Everyone! Get back to your positions! Scotty, outside of the room. Bridesmaids, inside!" Lori instructed the crowd.

"Oh, Nikki! Can I enter?" Scotty sung a few seconds later.

"Come in, Scotty!"

When he walked inside, Nikki had her back to him. Once he entered, she turned dramatically. He put his hands to his mouth and gasped. If one didn't witness the drama before, they'd think this was the first time he was seeing his bride.

"You look so beautiful, babe," Scotty whispered. He tried to kiss her, but she pulled away.

With a confused look, he stared at her.

"You're going to smudge my lipstick," Nikki whispered into his ear so that the others couldn't hear her. Scotty just smiled and tried to hug her, but she pulled away once again.

"My hair, Scotty," she whispered again.

Without hesitation, he took her hands in his. He had invested too much into this wedding to be spooked by the bizarre behavior of Nikki. First of all, weddings were expensive. And weddings based on the ideals of women like Nikki were even more expensive. Second of all, he was thirty-one—his parents had been bugging him to get married for years.

Scotty had met Nikki at the perfect time. She was the kind of girl who had dreamt about getting married ever since she was a little girl. Sure, he'd known her for only five months. But she was pretty, and she was ready, and that was all he needed.

"Alright! Before we head over to the church, how about we have a drink to calm our nerves?" Scotty asked his fiancé enthusiastically.

"Why not?" Nikki answered. For the first time, they actually agreed on something.

Demi rushed to pour them a drink.

"What do you want to drink, Nikki?" she asked.

"Hmm… Let's open the expensive wine that Scotty's parents got for us," she answered after a second.

"Are you sure? It's… red," Demi asked carefully.

"Yes, I'm sure," Nikki hissed through pressed lips, with a tone that didn't tolerate any back talk.

Demi then handed them the glasses with rigid fingers.

"Here's to a wonderful day ahead of us, darling." Scotty toasted and clinked his glass to hers. But her glass was too full. Her grip was too loose. Consequently, a few drops ended up right where they absolutely shouldn't… on Nikki's white dress.

Now, it's safe to say that every bride would've deemed this as the worst thing that could have happened to her on her wedding day. She had carefully selected the most beautiful dress according to her taste, and everyone was going to comment on it. And Nikki was no different. Okay, maybe a little different.

A second of sheer terror silenced the room, and everyone looked away as if direct contact with Nikki would turn them into stone.

"What have you done?!" Nikki screamed as angry tears started pouring down her cheeks like a waterfall.

"I'm sorry, I'm sorry, I'm so sorry," Scotty repeated weakly, suddenly losing his voice.

Nikki threw the glass of red wine in his face.

"I'm sure you are!" she yelled again, running out of the room.

Without words, Demi handed him a napkin. He brushed his face and finally looked like he was done. He stormed out, this time, without following her.

After fifteen minutes, while everyone tried to keep busy with anything they could find, Nikki came out of the bathroom. To her surprise, nobody was standing in front of the door.

Demi approached her carefully.

"The stain is barely visible." She treaded lightly.

"Don't lie to me. Of course, it's visible. But I can edit it out of the photos." Then she looked around the room. "Where's Scotty?"

"He left," Demi replied.

"I'm sure he went to the church… to give me time to get myself ready."

"Probably. I mean, definitely!"

"Come on, everyone! Everything's fine; let's head over to the church!" Nikki chimed out to the rest of her guests.

But nobody except for her was convinced that all was fine. Did Nikki have amnesia? Had she forgotten that she'd just thrown her drink in Scotty's face? However, it was too late now to not go along with what she'd asked of them.

In silence, the bridal party left Nikki's house and drove to the church. Inside the car, Nikki used this opportunity to catch up on her social media stories.

"Hi, guys! I hope you liked the photo I just posted of my dress! Scotty couldn't be more surprised! Of course, you'll see the video tonight! We're heading to the church now, and I must admit, I'm getting so nervous!" Nikki chirped, talking with the imaginary audience that existed inside her phone. "Girls, say hi!" She turned her phone to her bridesmaids, who waved and blew kisses like obedient soldiers.

That's the thing about girlfriends; they always stick with you.

"We're here," the driver said as he pulled up in front of the church.

The bridesmaids helped Nikki and her puffy dress get out of the car. She looked like a giant cupcake.

The view that welcomed them left them all breathless. Set in a quiet neighborhood, the church was quaint and beautiful. The yard was well-kept, and different types of flowers were everywhere. The sun was bright, and a gentle wind tickled their faces. The scenery made everyone feel calmer, Nikki included.

She finally understood why she was there. It was her wedding day, and she wasn't going to let the little things get in the way anymore.

"Demi, can you take my phone and put it in your purse, please?" she asked her best friend with a deep, calm inhale.

Pleasantly surprised, Demi took the phone with a sigh of relief.

"Shall we?" Nikki asked, and they all nodded in agreement. At that exact moment, the church bells started to ring.

Nikki smiled in anticipation, happy to see her future husband. In just an hour, they'd be husband and wife. Her perfect knight in shining armor. Sure, the morning had been anything but ideal. Everyone had warned her that weddings were stressful, but Nikki was delusional to believe that she'd be calm.

Feeling like a princess, she entered the church.

To her surprise, the only person by the altar was the priest. Not Scotty nor anyone from his family were there. *Where were they?* Scotty had left at least half an hour before them.

"Where is he?" she asked Demi, who just shook her head with worry. "Give me my phone, now!"

With shaky fingers, Nikki dialed Scotty's number. After three long rings, he picked up. But there wasn't any kind of greeting. Only silence.

"Scotty? Why aren't you here yet?"

A long silence followed.

"Nikki… I… I'm not coming," he answered, finally.

"What do you mean you're not coming? Get over here immediately!"

"No, I'm not coming. This is too much for me. *You* are too much for me. I can't marry you."

Nikki looked around the church at all the people who were staring at her in anticipation. She smiled at them and moved further away from them.

"Scotty, you can't do this to me. I already announced that we're getting married on social media. What will I tell people?"

A scoff and cold laugh followed, and then Scotty hung up on her. Nikki stared blankly at her phone for a few seconds before she ran away, crying for the third time that day.

CHAPTER 5

*N*ikki barely slept the night after she was left at the altar.

In a furious haze fueled by the rest of the wine that Scotty's parents had given them, she took the dress off and cut it up into long thin strips that she threw in her bathtub. Then she poured the second bottle of red wine that Scotty's parents had given them all over the dress. Of course, she listened to sad breakup songs during this private execution of her wedding gown. Did she feel any remorse for ruining a wedding dress that was worth more than a car? Not at all. Scotty had paid for it.

And it helped her more than any therapist ever could. Tired and sad, she eventually fell asleep in her bathtub, using the dress as a soggy blanket. The last thought in her head before she fell asleep was that red wine was good for the skin.

IN THE LIGHT of the morning, Nikki realized just how ridiculous she'd been the night before. She could have returned the dress, gotten the money back, and bought herself some new clothes. Why'd she allow her emotions to take the steering wheel?

Oh, well.

With great effort, Nikki got out of the bathtub, her back sore and her joints complaining after being in the same position for so long. She stretched out a little, trying to get some blood pumping in her numb toes.

Then she gathered the remains of the dress, put them in a black garbage bag, and wearing her over-sized sunglasses and pajamas, she went to throw it into the container bin outside.

Afterwards, Nikki decided to deal with the night-mare in the way most celebrities would—by reciting an ambiguous speech on her stories and explaining to her followers what had happened. It was something that would be gone, and hopefully, mostly forgotten in twenty-four hours, along with all the photos from the wedding. But before doing that, she had to make sure she looked fabulous.

Once she was done with the dress, Nikki returned back into the apartment and threw open her closet door. She picked the perfect outfit for her public appearance—a black and white dress shirt and dark jeans with some cute Jimmy Choo imitation shoes.

Next, she fixed her wedding hair. It was still gorgeous, so it wasn't that hard to pin a few loose strands here and there, and make it look a hundred percent again. At least, she didn't have to get ready all over again.

Her makeup hadn't been so lucky, though. All that crying had turned her face into a watercolor painting, finished with rosy cheeks and swollen eyes. After a quick skincare routine and light blush, Nikki put her sunglasses back on and pressed *live*.

"Hi, guys! Your girl, Nikki, here. I have some sad news for y'all. The wedding got canceled. I won't go into much detail except to say… Scotty is a coward and a spoiled man-child. He left me at the altar because he wasn't man enough to go through with it," she blurted the words out before she could stop herself. A little panicked and realizing that she was live, and there wasn't a delete button, she tried to wrap it up.

And quickly!

"I've decided to take some time off social media

to heal my heart. But I will be back soon. Thanks for understanding. Bye!" Nikki finished impulsively.

What have I done? Take some time off? Am I insane? I'll lose followers by the minute! But it was too late. She had allowed her heart to speak.

And her heart wanted to heal. Needed to heal.

Nikki felt the tears surge up her throat, and that terrified her. She was… alone. Completely alone. Left at the altar by the only man who had decided to commit to her. She had never felt so low and alone in her life, and she was unsure of how to deal with it.

But Nikki wasn't the kind of girl to wallow in self-pity for long. Nikki was worth a million bucks, she reminded herself. And if Scotty was too blinded by one small outburst to see that, then that was his loss, not hers.

With determination, she got up and decided to not let a beautiful outfit go by unnoticed. Nikki reached for her phone to take a selfie and upload it to social media, but then remembered that she had just told her followers that she was taking some time off. Already regretting it, she put her phone in her bag instead.

There were other ways to get an outfit noticed. And going out into the world was one of them.

So, that's what Nikki did.

NIKKI TRIED to force herself to call Demi or her parents back, but she just couldn't deal with their pity or questions. Her mind wasn't made up about anything yet.

The memory of her wedding day was a blur, but a painful one.

Leaving the apartment felt like a little self-care, something Nikki was used to doing almost on the daily. So out she went, heading to a few of her favorite spots—places she'd never been with Scotty.

Inside her favorite coffee house, the barista didn't know about her wedding fiasco, and she greeted her with the usual customer-designated smile. That's just what she needed.

"One large tea. With a shot of rum inside." Nikki didn't care that it was still three in the afternoon. She needed it. Or so she told herself.

"Coming right up," the barista exclaimed, her face void of emotion.

A minute later, with the tea in her hand, Nikki walked around the city aimlessly. She walked past a few of the shops that she usually went into, but didn't feel like walking in. So, on she went.

Walking.

Sulking.

Due to her empty stomach, the rum warmed her body more than it usually would've. The alcohol also released her emotions, and the depressing autumn weather made her feel even more lonely.

The only person she really wanted to talk to

was… Scotty. Nikki felt the tears fall down her face before she could stop them.

Suddenly, a loud, anxious bark took her attention away from her sadness. She turned to her right, just in time to see a small yorkie barking at her from a pet shop window. He was bearing his teeth as if he were a huge predator, when in reality, he was petite and almost adorable-looking.

The dog looked… angry. That was it. But due to its size, the anger looked silly and made Nikki smile through her tears.

"Hey, buddy." She tapped the glass gently, phantom-petting the dog through the glass of the storefront. That only caused more anger in the little creature, who barked and yelped, bearing its teeth again and scratching at the glass.

"You're coming home with me," Nikki whispered to herself, walking straight into the shop without stopping to think about it.

"Hi, welcome," an enthusiastic teenager greeted her.

"Hi!" Nikki felt all the emotion she had lost flood back into her, a little happiness, a little spark of joy. "I just… just…"

She pointed back to the store window, and then stopped when the girl took her hand to her chest and stared at her.

"Oh, sorry, but… Are you… Nikki with an I? The influencer?" chirped the acne-faced, oily-haired girl.

Always happy to meet a fan, Nikki's face lit up.

Actually, this was her first real-life fan. On the day she decided to take a break from social media, things were starting to look up, and she had a bit of mixed feelings about it all.

"Why, yes, I am!" she exclaimed with her best practiced smile. "What's your name?"

"I'm Annie! You won't believe how excited I am to meet you! Can we take a selfie together? Please?"

"Sure!" Nikki chanted, overjoyed, yet she tried to keep her cool. *Someday, when I have thousands of fans stopping me, even at the grocery store, I'll remember Annie, my first real-life fan.* Nikki blew a kiss as Annie's shaky fingers took the picture.

"So… Nikki, what can I do for you?" the girl asked after the deed was done.

"I'd like to purchase that small dog at the front. The yorkie." Nikki smiled, feeling a little giddy with the turn the day had taken.

"Sure. That's a male yorkie, and he's only three months old," the girl explained.

"Perfect! I need a collar as well. Something shiny," Nikki said with dreamy eyes. A cure for her loneliness. The little yorkie was exactly what she needed.

"That's a great idea! We actually have personalized, bedazzled collars with the puppy's name. Would you like one of those?" Annie asked.

"That sounds fabulous!" Nikki answered, picturing all the social media posts and the views they'd receive. The yorkie would help her brand. A lot.

"Have you picked out a name already?" the girl asked as she rang up the order on the register.

"Hmm… let's go with… Scotty," Nikki answered after a few minutes of silence.

An awkward silence followed as the girl's smile faded, and the happiness was gone from her eyes. At that moment, Nikki realized that the girl must have seen her live video. If she was truly a fan, she'd know everything about Scotty.

"It's a joke!" Nikki laughed nervously. "I thought it would be fun!"

The girl just nodded with a smile and went to get the yorkie and the collar.

"Okay, Nikki. That'll be twelve hundred dollars," the girl said nonchalantly.

Shock shot down Nikki's spine. *Twelve hundred? For a dog?*

"Maybe I can post a promotional story and a post with the dog, and you can just give him to me for… free?" she asked enthusiastically. "Could do a great deal of showing around the store, too, tag you every time I upload pictures of Scotty for the next month or so," she added with her biggest smile.

"Oh, no, I'm sorry. I can't do that. My father is the owner, and he has a strict policy about influencers."

Nikki felt her heart fall to her feet. "And what would that policy be?"

"He doesn't believe in influencers," Annie blurted out even faster.

Embarrassed and angry, Nikki opened her wallet to evaluate her financial situation. She really needed Scotty. The dog—that was.

That's when she noticed Scotty's—the man—credit card. It was still in her wallet since Scotty had given it to her to pay the caterers for the party that never was.

A barely noticeable ping of guilt pinched Nikki's heart. The dog cost almost as much as her wedding shoes had cost her, which Scotty also paid for. But… Scotty was rich. Would he even notice a tiny thousand missing from his account?

Nikki justified the yorkie purchase with a personal pledge to cut the card in half once she got home. And even if Scotty noticed, what would he do? Call her and yell at her? He left her at the altar! Gifting her this dog was the least he could do! Nikki was sure he'd think so.

"There you go," Nikki said and handed over the card.

Ten minutes later, Nikki and Scotty were out on the street. The sun seemed brighter than before. Scotty was pulling on the collar like crazy. And Nikki wasn't lonely anymore.

A week later, Nikki considered herself strong enough to face people.

"I was devastated about the wedding. I just stared

at the wall when I got home," Demi said to her one day, visiting Nikki's apartment. "You and Scotty... you seemed perfect together. What do you think got into him?"

"You see, Demi, Scotty was always an asshole," Nikki replied with as much calm as she could muster. "I just refused to see that. A rich, pompous asshole. No man can be trusted. Well, expect... Scotty."

Demi looked at her with confusion before realizing that she was talking about the small, angry dog on her lap. It was chewing on the end of her shirt, and she didn't seem to care.

"You named the dog... Scotty?" she asked in terror. "Nikki... are you alright?"

"What?! Am I not allowed to joke about this? It's my coping mechanism! The name just came out. And he," she said, pointing at the dog, "doesn't seem to respond to anything else. He *is* a Scotty, after all."

"I guess it *is* funny," Demi replied. She took a sip of her coffee, observing Nikki's small but tidy apartment. "And have you heard from him? Scotty the man?"

"I blocked his number," Nikki answered.

She hadn't. But she could never admit to Demi that *he* had blocked *her*. He hadn't answered any of her drunken messages. Well, except for one. The one that came an hour after Scotty the yorkie was hers.

I can't believe you, Nikki! YOU BOUGHT A DOG?! With my CREDIT CARD? I have been with many crazy women, who have done many crazy things, but this one takes the cake! I am so glad I never married you! Consider that fucking dog a parting gift, and a bribe to never contact me again!

When Nikki got this message, she deleted it immediately. From her phone and from her memory. Scotty was just angry that she bought the dog.

He didn't mean it, she told herself.

TURNED OUT, Scotty *did* mean it. He never called her again. It had been five months since the wedding, and spring was just around the corner.

Eventually, Nikki did go back to social media. After her public meltdown, her following increased. The drama attracted people. She still couldn't reach a thousand, but she was back to doing what she loved.

Scotty the dog was now eight months old, and his anger issues seemed to mellow out as he grew older. His favorite place to sleep was on the bed next to Nikki. Maybe it was the dog, or maybe she was too hurt from the wedding drama, but Nikki hadn't been on any dates since. She couldn't recognize herself anymore, the once-fun Nikki who used to go out every Friday and Saturday night, and booked a date for the work week as well.

Now, she focused on her career, her dog, and fashion.

Before and after the failed wedding, Nikki had done a little bit of work on the side here and there, too. After getting fired, she hadn't gotten a new job, but survived doing the odd dress orders from time to time, her name going from mouth to mouth, and clients contacting her through email.

Demi had insisted a few times that Nikki should open up a new social media account or even a webpage for her dresses and crafts, but she didn't think it was worth it. She wasn't that good, and after all, dressmaking was more of a hobby that was paying her bills. Between prom dresses, graduation ones, and the odd girl wanting to upstage her friends at a quinceañera, she had enough to pay her rent and bills.

Well, Scotty's money had helped, too. The man. Scotty used to pay for most of the meals, for all of her clothes, and a few other things that Nikki had indulged in.

But now he was gone, and it meant that Nikki was back to spending most of her time on growing her social media account, which had become stagnant at almost a thousand followers. *Almost* being the keyword.

So, dresses it was. Nikki had told all her friends, neighbors, and even shop owner acquaintances that she was making dresses, and any order was welcomed… Her mistake.

"A wedding dress? What?" Nikki stammered, speaking at an irregularly fast rate.

"A custom wedding dress," Demi replied, a huge smile on her face as she stood at the door of Nikki's apartment.

Nikki waved her in, speechless, and Demi went on to explain that one of her sister's friends had seen one of her quinceañera dresses at a cousin's party, and she was fascinated by the work.

She wanted Nikki to make her wedding dress, which was in about nine months. She had even sent Demi a few pictures of her ideas so she could be the one to go to Nikki and ask for it, as the bride-to-be hadn't found out that Nikki was the one to have made that dress until speaking with Demi's sister later on. It had been a game of mouth to mouth, a weird network of people asking around until the bride had found Nikki. Most would have thought it was destiny, the opportunity of a lifetime.

But not Nikki.

As she stared at the wedding gown pictures that Demi was showing her, Scotty running around the apartment and barking at Demi's shoes, Nikki's blood ran cold.

"No," she said.

Demi paled a little.

"No? What do you mean, Nikki? This is the opportunity of a lifetime!. This could kick start your own wedding dress business or something! The woman has contacts, Nikki. Friends with money who will see the dress."

"I said no, Demi!" Nikki snapped, pushing Demi to the side and walking toward her back window. "You should go now."

"Nikki, why are you being like this?" Demi wondered, her voice a little softer, a little scared.

"I. Said. Go. NOW!" Each word was a slap, and each of them were directed at the window as Nikki didn't even turn around.

Quietly, Demi walked away, and Nikki let one frustrated tear run down her cheek before wiping it away and finding a cute filter to take a selfie with.

She was no dressmaker. And she wasn't ready to disappoint anyone else. She had already disappointed herself with the whole fake wedding thing. No. There was no way that Nikki was getting involved with weddings again.

Never again.

CHAPTER 6

*I*t was a warm morning when Nikki got the most exciting news of her life.

You have been invited to "How to increase your following and become more fabulous by the minute." The email read.

Squealing with excitement, Nikki went on to read all the information of an event she had heard lots about. It was more like a masterclass, held by none other than Marie Davidson, her idol. Nikki had been a part of her newsletter for a long time, and she guessed that was why she had gotten the exclusive invitation to the event of the year.

Marie was just a regular girl who'd started off the same way as Nikki, with less than a hundred followers. Marie now had a hundred thousand followers, and she promoted some of the most famous brands, many of which Nikki loved and often purchased whenever she could.

Maria was everything Nikki wished she could be. Her dream came true. She had it all, and she was the kind of person Nikki had to befriend, and whose wisdom she had to learn from in order to get every-thing she desired.

So, a few weeks after the invitation arrived, Nikki borrowed the thousand-dollar fee from her parents (after a fair amount of begging), carefully planned and chose all her outfits for the three-day retreat, put Scotty in his doggy stroller, and then she was off.

Off to get everything she had always wanted.

THE EVENT TOOK place inside a picturesque landscape, Hotel Dogma, on the shore of a lovely lake. There were scenic paths that encircled the lake, and spring really brought out the best from the surrounding nature. Upon arriving after the long bus ride, Nikki immediately knew that she was at the right place.

Until she walked into the hotel.

"No pets allowed in our hotel," the older man at the reception said when she walked up to the counter to check in. His hairline was receding, and his blazer was just as old as he was, making Nikki scowl at it.

She just rolled her eyes, taking his age to be the biggest factor for this outburst.

Nowadays, every hotel should accept pets! Nikki thought.

"Sir, can I please speak with your manager?" she asked calmly.

"I *am* the manager," the man replied in a curt, but stern, tone. "And we don't allow pets in our hotel," he said again patiently.

"What am I supposed to do with my precious baby, then?" Nikki shrieked. "We're over three hours away from home! I can't possibly go back there and come back before the retreat starts! The fee for this event was a thousand dollars!" She snapped at the innocent man. "I don't expect you to understand, but I will lose all my valuable time with Marie just because of your incompetence and your stupid hotel rules!"

Nikki let a single tear down her cheek—this was her first defense against men. But the receptionist wasn't having it.

"Please, lady, there's no need for tears," he said in the same calm and regular tone. "There is actually an animal shelter next to the hotel, and I'm sure they'll allow you to leave the dog there during your stay," he explained, pointing to the side of the hotel that she was meant to go toward.

"Animal shelter?" Nikki felt herself pale. "This is a twelve-hundred-dollar dog! Scotty doesn't belong in an animal shelter!"

The receptionist seemed a little fed up. He turned his attention to the computer, almost ignoring Nikki as he typed.

"You could try some of the sitters, but they're far away and often booked out months in advance. So, either take it to the shelter, or go back home. Unfortunately, those are the only options," the man simply answered, his eyes no longer on Nikki.

"Please! Let me keep him in my room! He's my emotional support dog! You won't even know he's there."

The receptionist lifted his gaze from the computer in disbelief.

"You need a certification to support that claim," he replied without emotion. "Do you have it?"

"Your complete disregard about the life of pets disgusts me!" Nikki screamed dramatically, then she spun around and headed to the door.

Still feeling like she'd won the fight, she looked at the receptionist again before walking out the door.

"Follow the path on the left. The animal shelter will be on your right," he said without looking up, reading her mind.

Leaving Scotty at the animal shelter was devastating. He looked at her with his tiny, angry eyes, and Nikki cried as she walked away. This time, for real. The girl who worked there was completely understanding about her situation, and agreed how terrible the receptionist had been. She was a girl in her late teens and very passionate about animal rescue.

Nikki liked her.

Arriving in her room moments later, Nikki fixed her makeup, but still felt like a part of her was missing.

I'll visit Scotty every chance I get, on every break I have, she thought.

THE RETREAT WAS INCREDIBLE. Nikki was learning so much that by the end of day two, her notebook was full, and she had to go to the small gift shop in the hotel to buy another one.

She even got a chance to speak with Marie herself, even though it lasted for only a minute. But Nikki knew how busy Marie was, so that minute felt like a lifetime for her.

One day, I'll have the same problem.

Marie spoke a lot about manifesting and visualizing goals. She told them that the biggest contributor to her success was the power of her mind. She spoke in great length about her story, about the techniques they could use to visualize what they were after, and how to plan and write down all the things they wanted and needed. She also gave them tools to use on their social media, many of which Nikki already knew, and many more she hadn't heard about before.

And Nikki was soaking it all in.

"To be the person you want to be, you have to create that person in your head first," Marie said on the last day while giving a lecture that was being recorded live.

From then on, and starting that very first day, Nikki knew she'd have to visualize her perfect life, both in the morning before getting up, and every evening before going to bed.

That first morning at the retreat, Nikki visualized a thousand followers, how that would feel, the messages she would receive from brands, and the photos she would post promoting their products. She did the same at night, and then repeated the same every morning of the retreat.

Once, a tiny thought about love slipped through. Scotty the man had broken her heart, but Nikki was a strong believer of love. And she deserved to be happy.

So, on the third morning, she allowed herself to visualize a handsome man who was dressed impeccably, who was rich, and who understood her. Who wasn't spooked by her career, or how impatient and angry she sometimes got.

And most importantly, someone who would love Scotty the dog like he was his own.

BY THE THIRD AFTERNOON, when the masterclasses were almost over, Nikki felt like a completely new person.

That was, until the girl from the shelter rushed into the hotel during their early dinner. She frantically searched for Nikki, finding her close to the buffet, sitting next to Marie. Somehow, Nikki had managed to strike up somewhat of a friendship with her idol, and they were eating side-by-side, with matching salads on their plates.

"Nikki! I've been looking everywhere for you!" The girl panted, putting her hands on her knees and looking utterly distressed. "Scotty ran away!"

Nikki's world fell apart within a second. Trying to stand up, she felt like she was going to faint, and a shriek interrupted the peaceful atmosphere in the room.

"How could you?" She managed to squeal. "I trusted you with the most valuable thing I own! And you... you lost him?!"

The girl started crying then, and everyone's attention shifted to them both.

"I'm so sorry. I must have forgotten to lock his gate after play time this afternoon... and he escaped when we were taking the bigger dogs out for a walk before dinner! I am so sorry! I feel so guilty!" The girl spoke through her tears, and people whispered and pointed all around them.

Without a word, Nikki got up and pushed past the girl, heading straight for the exit.

In tears, Nikki ran alongside the path surrounding the lake, the afternoon light turning orange and pink, the sky a masterpiece of colors that Nikki ignored completely.

My little Scotty can't take care of himself in this wilderness! He hasn't spent a day alone outside in his entire life. What if there are wild animals in these woods? Scotty would make for a delicious dessert for them! Can I persuade the cops to issue an amber alert for a pet? Is that even a thing? Sure, it's only for children, but Scotty is my child!

At this thought, Nikki stopped running and started wailing near the lake. If Scotty died, she would be devastated. She could never survive losing him.

She sat down on the rocky shore, her face in her hands, trying to contain herself. She had to think, think like Scotty. Where would he go? What could she do to find him? But the fear she felt was like an ocean pressing against her eyes, her chest, her whole being. And all she could do was let it out.

"Miss?" a male voice suddenly interrupted her after what felt like forever.

She lifted her head to see a handsome man standing in front of her, a beautiful sunset spreading behind him and bathing him in a golden and marvelous light. He was tall, fit, and had big black eyes that were staring right at her.

Even dressed in his gym shorts, he looked fancy. If she wasn't so upset, she'd appreciate how beautiful the scenery looked, him with the background of the lake, and the sun trying to play hide-and-seek with the horizon.

"What's the matter?" he asked, handing her a tissue as he crouched down in front of her.

It was only then that Nikki realized how loud her sobs had been. There was compassion and under-standing behind his beautiful black eyes, and Nikki felt her heart shatter all over again. She didn't even know how to put it into words, or if she was even capable of it.

"My dog…," she started to say, but then noticed the two dogs arriving behind the man. A big one and a small one. And one of them was… "Scotty!"

She ran toward him and picked him up before he understood what was happening. She rubbed her face into the animal's fur, crying with a huge smile on her face while thanking the universe for bringing him back to her.

"Scotty, I'm so sorry for leaving you at that awful place! I will never leave you alone ever again! Oh, my precious, precious boy!" she whispered into his tiny, furry ears. Scotty seemed oblivious to the conundrum he had caused with his sudden departure from the animal shelter. He was just eager to be put back onto the ground.

The man watched the event with a grin as his giant dog came next to him and sat down, tail wagging.

"So, is this your dog, Scotty? I noticed the collar when he approached us. Such a mighty name for such a small fellow! I was taking Yardley here for our usual afternoon walk when little Scotty met us. I'm telling you, it was love at first sight! They've been playing with each other all afternoon! I thought we'd walk a bit more in case we ran into the owner. And I guess we did."

Nikki smiled through her tears. Scotty was a little angry furball that hated everyone, so Yardley had to be one special dog for him to not be his grumpy self.

"I was so worried. You have no idea how much you've helped me by keeping him safe," Nikki whispered, feeling self-conscious and embarrassed about everything that had happened. "I'm going through a rough time, and Scotty has been my biggest supporter," she admitted.

"I get it," the man replied. "I'm going through a divorce myself. Yardley here has been my biggest cheerleader." The man was silent for a moment, both of them lost in each other's eyes before he spoke again. "Hey, why don't we grab some coffee or tea to celebrate the lucky return of Scotty? You've had dinner already, right? Otherwise, it could be dinner. What do you say?"

"A hot drink sounds lovely," Nikki replied with a shy smile, realizing that this might be some kind of a date. She didn't want to get her hopes up, though, but the man seemed like a decent person.

"I'm Liam, by the way," he said as he walked alongside her, pointing to a cottage in the distance. "And that over there is my place."

"I'm Nikki. With an I," she said.

Happy to be in the company of such a handsome man and relieved to have found Scotty, Nikki let out a relieved sigh.

The view over the lake was getting more and more beautiful by the second, so she walked alongside it, with Liam on one side and Scotty on the other.

CHAPTER 7

*L*iam and Nikki exchanged numbers and socials that first afternoon by the lake, with hot mugs of tea in their hands, and had been chatting ever since. It'd been a couple of weeks since that first encounter. And even though they hadn't seen each other that often, living over three hours apart, they still talked to each other daily.

Usual things like, "How's work?" or "If you're not

too busy, maybe we can meet up for coffee and a walk over the weekend."

They also met up a couple times for coffee at a small café halfway between Nikki's apartment and his cottage home by the lake, a compromise to avoid having one person travel the entire distance. Nikki had never done long-distance dating before, and she wasn't sure how much she could keep up at it, but there was something about Liam…

Nikki was noticing small things about him that she had never noticed about any other man. For example, how he would play with his nails if he were nervous, how he spoke very softly to the servers in the café and was always patient with them, how he would try to hide if something was bothering him by letting Nikki take over the conversation. And how he wholeheartedly listened to anything Nikki had to say. And Nikki talked a lot, that's for sure.

Having her morning coffee by the window with Scotty sitting on her lap one morning, she wondered if he'd noticed things about her, too. Or if he was thinking about her the same way she was.

Almost as if listening, her phone rang.

"Hello?" she answered sheepishly.

"Hey, Nikki, how's your morning going? Did you sleep alright?"

"Hey, Liam, yeah. I did. Scotty snuggled by me all night. It was great."

"I'm a little jealous…" At Nikki's weird snort of a chuckle, Liam clarified. "Yardley slept with me also, but he took up most of the bed. I woke up with such a bad back ache that I had to do an hour of yoga just to correct my posture."

After that, Liam went on to tell her how long he'd been practicing yoga for, and how good it'd been for his health. For a change, Nikki listened, and she even agreed to try the discipline one of these days. Maybe it'd be good for her socials—showing that she exercised and cared about the way she felt and looked.

Before ending the call, they agreed to see each other next weekend, and Nikki would go over to the cottage again for a couple of days, in which Liam promised that he'd show her how to properly do yoga so she wouldn't injure herself.

But before the week was over, Nikki had to go shopping, as yoga appropriate pants weren't part of her usual wardrobe.

During the week, Nikki worked on a few more dress orders, feeling a little better about everything, even about how the dresses were coming out. And by the time the weekend rolled around, she was excited about the prospect of spending an entire weekend with Liam.

DURING THE TRIP to the cottage, Nikki reflected back on her parents' relationship, thinking about everything she had always aspired to have. Without fail, her father always made sure that he made her mother feel like she was enough, and that she was doing a great job—despite not having everything completely figured out.

And Nikki's mother was the same, making sure to comfort him whenever he was stressed by talking about what was wrong with him. She remembered that whenever her mother was stressed, her father would take young Nikki out for the day to allow her mother to have time to herself, to do some self-care, and when they got back, her parents would always hug like they haven't seen each other for days, and then talk about everything they've done during their time apart.

Right then, Nikki realized that she'd never settle unless she had what they had. Attempting a life with Scotty the man had been the biggest mistake of her life. She wanted that type of soft, attentive, caring, and comforting love. She wanted it all.

Nikki often thought about how uncommon men like her father were. Actually, she'd asked him about it once. And her father replied with, "Nikki, there aren't a lot of men who start out the way that I am now. Before I met your mother, I would cheat on my girl-friends and avoid putting any effort into the relation-ship. But there was something different about your mother, something that forced me to start caring and paying attention. That thing is called love, and I had a heart full of it for her. If a man truly loves you, he will put in as much effort and care into your relationship as your mother and I. Don't settle for anything less."

She almost had. Thinking back on it, her father hadn't looked delighted about her engagement with Scotty. He tried to give her the freedom to choose, but she could see now that he had never been pleased with her choice. She wondered if he'd be different if he met Liam. *When* he met Liam.

"So great to have you back," Liam said when he picked her up from the terminal, planting a kiss on her forehead. He then picked up Scotty the dog, and placed him gently in the back of his car with Yardley before opening the door for Nikki.

She had taken a few videos and shots of the trip that she had already posted, and she felt a little nervous as she looked at Liam once he was back at the wheel.

"Mind if I take a photo for my stories?" she asked. She'd never been one to ask before, but there was something a little different about Liam. And his approval would mean everything for her. A make-or-break situation.

"Of course!" Liam exclaimed, putting his head next to hers and smiling even before she had the camera ready.

He even waited for her to choose the perfect filter and caption before starting the car, and Nikki smiled from ear-to-ear as they drove.

"ARE WE IN ONE?" Nikki whispered. She only prayed that Liam had heard her, and she wouldn't have to repeat herself.

They had been talking about relationships for a while, Liam telling her about his failed marriage, his divorce, and how much he had suffered through it. And Nikki had shared her bad experience with Scotty the man.

Liam had been very understanding, and he'd told Nikki that she deserved something better, that Scotty the man had clearly not been the one for her.

So impulsively, Nikki asked him if what they had was a relationship. Yes, they had been sort of dating for a while now, but they never gave it a label, and she wasn't sure what they were. She was jumping in, something she had never done so outright as she always waited for the man to take the major steps.

"Us? In a relationship?" Liam asked softly. He then paused, waiting for Nikki to say something, but she simply nodded. "Nikki… I would love to try a relationship with you. I know this long-distance dating thing hasn't been the easiest for either of us, and I don't know what label we might've had until now, but I'd love to call you my girlfriend. We haven't known each other that long, but I feel like we have lifetimes to spend together. Whenever I'm with you, I unintentionally start smiling. I can feel my heart speed up inside my chest, and you make me laugh so easily."

Nikki beamed at him, and she felt happy tears threatening to come out. She never cried out of happiness before, so she held it in, not ready for another first in her life.

"I feel exactly the same," she replied.

IT WAS a weekend later that Liam went to Nikki's apartment for the first time. She was so nervous that she cleaned the entire place three times, and made the best effort possible to clean up the mess of fabrics and beads scattered around her small studio. Finally, she decided to just close that door and keep it that way, hoping Liam wouldn't ask about it.

But of course, he asked about it.

"What's behind the mysterious door?" he asked after Nikki gave him a little tour of the place, completely avoiding the close door.

"Oh, nothing... just... you know... laundry room."

"Are there dirty undies in there that I can't see?" Liam joked, slowly moving toward the door.

"No, there's just... erm... drugs!" Nikki blurted. Her cheeks turned dark red, and she cursed herself internally.

"Do you have an indoor garden there?" Liam asked again with a chuckle. "You know, it's okay with me. There's nothing you can show me that will scare me away. I want to know you, Nikki, truly know you," he explained softly.

And that did it. Moving slowly toward the door

and without saying words, she opened it and turned on the light, motioning for Liam to walk in.

She was terrified of the look she would see on his face, but was oddly delighted and equally scared when his eyes lit up with excitement, looking at all the half-made dresses scattered around the small room.

"Nikki… did you make all of this?"

"Well… yes. It's just a small hustle that pays my bills while I wait for the whole influencer thing to really get going."

She had almost two thousand followers now, with plenty of small brands reaching out to her, but she was still far from making enough money to make a living out of it. Just enough to pay the odd bill here and there while the dresses paid the rent and groceries.

"Nikki, this is fantastic! You have a wonderful eye for fashion, and your details are… I don't have words for it," Liam exclaimed as he ran his fingers down the hem of a hand-beaded skirt. "This is amazing; you have so much talent!"

"Really?" That was all Nikki could say.

"Really, Nikki. Take it from someone who has started many businesses throughout his life, and who knows talent when he sees it. You have such a *gift*! Why don't you share these on social media? I only ever see you show designer and branded clothes. Why don't you show your own?"

At that moment, Nikki felt a little more confident in herself. She wasn't sure whether she was ready to show her dresses, but maybe she could start showing some of the everyday clothes she had started making for herself with the leftover bits of fabric she always got from her dresses.

Taking one of those everyday skirts out of her closet later on and telling Liam about what she was thinking, she put it on and twirled for him.

"What do you think?" she asked.

"I think you should be in charge of all fashion from now on. Every single fashion company should be under your jurisdiction. You're amazing," he stated.

Nikki was flattered and smiled at his words, thinking about the possibilities of what she could have.

THAT NIGHT, they got takeout for dinner, and then Nikki helped Liam sort out the couch for him to stay the night. It was his first time in her apartment, so naturally, it was also his first time staying over. He had insisted that the couch was perfect, so Nikki grabbed some spare sheets and blankets for him.

As they finished, she sat by his side and gazed into his eyes, smiling mindlessly. Liam gently reclined his face toward Nikki's and pecked her forehead softly before shifting his lips to hers and locking them with grace.

His breath felt hot inside her mouth.

She was melting.

The kiss must've lasted about a minute, neither of them wanting to separate, but eventually, they remembered that they needed oxygen.

"Good night, Nikki," Liam said, a little out of breath. And before she did something she might or might not regret, Nikki retreated to her bedroom and closed the door a little too forcefully.

Lying on her bed, her thoughts lingered on him. Her eyes closed, and Nikki let herself continue to dream about Liam throughout the night.

few days after Liam stayed over, Nikki woke up missing him, but with renewed energy and a feeling that she could conquer the world. She was Nikki with an I, and the world was her oyster. Following Liam's advice, she had been brave enough to share one of her dresses online the morning prior, posing with it while having her morning coffee by the large window.

And her socials had blown over.

People loved her dress!

She was excited to surprise him, and so she packed a small bag with some snacks that she knew Liam loved and some treats for the dogs, too. She then put Scotty in his carrier and took a cab to the station. She had her backpack hanging loosely from her shoulder, Scotty being carried on the other.

She also packed a full change of clothes in a hurry, just in case, as well as a little blanket for Scotty. She hoped her visit would be a peace offering of some sort, even though they weren't arguing or anything. Nikki just wanted to show Liam how much she cared about him, and how much he was changing her life.

The trip felt like it lasted an eternity with how excited Nikki was, but she didn't mind. Nikki used the time to check in on her social media, applying for new sponsorships as well as chatting with a few clients who had requested custom dresses over the past few days.

Once she arrived at the station, Nikki took a taxi to the hotel to make sure she surprised Liam. From there, she put Scotty on his leash and walked, enjoying the afternoon sun along the lake.

Everything was sparkles and rainbows until Nikki got to the path that led to Liam's house.

There, it all turned into electric storms and fury.

"Son of a bitch," she mumbled, digging her heels into the gravel to stop Scotty from running over. The little shit was tugging at the leash, and Nikki pulled back again and again until Scotty did a weird leap in the air, the leash flying from Nikki's hand.

Double betrayal.

"Not you, too!" she yelled after the dog.

Nikki watched as Liam swung on the porch's hammock with another woman, Scotty running toward them, and Yardley running toward Scotty. They weren't holding hands or anything like Nikki and Liam often did, but they were laughing together in very close proximity.

Nikki's body entered fight-or-flight mode, but she couldn't run away with Scotty almost to the porch now. Instead, Nikki went with the third option that wasn't as commonly expressed, freezing. Her eyes remained fixated on the pair; she surveyed Liam's every move, needing to know if he would also kiss that woman as he did with her.

He was sitting with his legs crossed, and he was quiet, meaning that he was listening to her speak. Nikki couldn't believe what she was seeing.

Her heart sank.

Her mind reeled, and she couldn't stop it for anything in the world. She couldn't think of another explanation other than that he was cheating on her. Feeling abandoned, Nikki had only a few unending seconds, barely a minute, before Liam noticed Scotty running to them, and he looked up.

Nikki could physically feel pieces of her heart falling apart; she couldn't take any more of it. Surfacing from the pit of her despair, she tried to turn around and run. But she couldn't leave Scotty.

"Scotty!" she yelled with all her strength in a

desperate attempt to have him return so they could run away together.

But Scotty was now with Yardley, both of them running around like old friends.

"Traitor," she mumbled.

Unable to run away, Nikki stood there as Liam looked up, a huge smile on his face when he recognized her.

Why is he smiling?

He said something to the woman by his side, and when he saw that Nikki wasn't moving, he started walking toward her instead, his expression changing to concern when he noticed how distressed she was.

When he was only a few steps away, he called out to her.

"Nikki! Why are you standing there? Is everything okay?"

Is everything okay? Is everything okay?!

Nikki balled her fists, trying to keep the anger in. She wouldn't be a bridezilla again. She wouldn't let all that anger control her. Taking in one of the deep breaths that Liam had taught her in yoga, she tried to control her emotions, but she couldn't keep them in.

"Who is she?" She snapped instead, her voice small and broken.

Liam looked over his shoulder, and then back to her.

"Her?"

Nikki may have nodded; she wasn't sure what her body was doing anymore.

"She's my sister," Liam said, taking the last step toward her. "Actually, she's my twin, and if you walk over to the house with me and get closer, you might even notice how much we look alike."

Liam smiled gently and reached his hand out to her.

A little reluctant, Nikki took it.

"Who did you think she was?" he asked, pulling her closer and breathing against her neck as he hugged her quickly.

"The worst," she replied, tears prickling in her eyes.

"I'm sorry that you've been led to think the worst of men. But not all of us are like that. I would never do something like that to you, Nikki. I was actually telling Mia all about you, and she'd love to meet you."

Wiping a rebellious tear off her cheek, Nikki grinned.

"It'll be nice to meet her, too."

AFTER TALKING to Mia for a while, Nikki decided that she needed to do a little more.

"You said you're going back to town tonight… Why don't you come over to my apartment?" Nikki offered.

"I'd love that!" Mia exclaimed as Liam returned with a cup of tea for them both. "I got my car here, so

I could give you a ride, too. It's way faster than the train or bus."

Mia smiled, and her expression was so similar to Liam's that she couldn't help the laughter that bubbled out of her. The twins were indeed pretty similar-looking.

To her surprise, Mia and Nikki were quite similar, too, in other ways. They both had a soft spot for fashion, and Mia even worked in fashion design before quitting to become a writer—she felt as though fashion design wasn't the career for her, more of a hobby. And she was also very present on social media, already asking to follow Nikki on the drive over to her place and talking about mutual influencers they both knew and admired.

Back at Nikki's place that night, while sharing one too many glasses of white wine, Nikki finally showed Mia some of her designs after she kept on insisting to see them.

"This is way better than anything I've even dreamt of making," she said with marvel in her voice.

"Really?" Nikki was a little drunk, but she was sure she heard Mia correctly.

"Honestly, Nikki, you have real talent. You have what people study for years and years to do. And you do it almost naturally, right?"

It was true. Nikki had never found fashion something to struggle over. She simply envisioned something and knew how to make it. It was something she had been doing for years, even if she didn't think she was good enough. But that was mostly because she didn't have any formal education, so she always felt like there was a lot she didn't know, and a lot she should study in order to be any good in the real word of fashion.

Most of what she learned had been by trial and error and watching people online, a few tutorials here and there, and plenty of hours of work.

"I guess…"

"Nikki, Liam told me a little about this, but he never told me just how good you are. Seriously, I think you should think about expanding your career in fashion; you're a natural!"

That night, Nikki couldn't sleep, thinking about her designs instead. After hours and hours of shifting in bed, when sleep didn't find her, she decided to get up and get to work again. And so, she designed.

She designed new everyday dresses that she could show on her socials—party dresses and even some casual wear she could use for her yoga practice, because she hadn't really liked anything she'd seen at the stores.

CHAPTER 9

Liam and Nikki had been dating for two months now, and everything felt like a dream. He showed his love through contact and would hold Nikki's hand wherever they went, and he often caressed her cheeks or hair, looking at her with adoring eyes. If they were facing each other, Liam would always stare at Nikki like a baby seeing a dog for the first time, and it made her blush every single time.

Nikki felt so comfortable around him, something she had never felt before, and it made her feel secure in a new and often scary way. She'd never felt like that.

Liam, with Mia's help, had also convinced Nikki to take her fashion design more seriously. She had started sharing her clothes more and more on social media, and it made her stats spike.

Quickly, she eventually hit the follower count that she'd been trying to reach for so long, and people started messaging her and praising her work and amazing sense of fashion.

On top of all that, Nikki was practicing yoga almost daily, Liam often joining her. Exercise had helped her with dealing with her emotions, and anger wasn't something she felt nowadays. Liam also taught her how to meditate, and the benefits were so obvious that Nikki wondered why she'd never tried it before. It'd been hard at first, but she was feeling better and better every day.

And then there was Liam himself. Her knight. He always flattered Nikki, sending her kind words that she sometimes thought she didn't even deserve. He only saw the best in her, and he made her want to be better. To *do* better.

Liam would always take the time to remember the small things and bring them up during conversations, asking about Nikki's joys and pleasures. And Nikki made sure to give him a lot of attention as well, taking notice of how he would always make sure he was on the roadside if they were walking on a narrow side-walk, how he would pet dogs that came up to him, and how he would always make way for elderly people and women.

Nikki tried to follow his example and become a better person, too, something she had never stopped to think about before, as she thought she was perfect as she was. It felt impossible not to be attracted to him. Like he was a magnet. Like he was everything that was right in Nikki's life.

And Liam had no problem appearing in Nikki's stories and posts either. He actually enjoyed the atten-tion. And her followers did, too. Liam worked as a software developer, and he understood the power of social media more than anyone.

Not that it mattered, since he was her soulmate, but Liam was also incredibly rich. He was self-made, just as Nikki hoped to be one day. That was the best kind of rich, unlike Scotty's inherited wealth. And Liam was pushing Nikki to achieve everything she wanted, helping her become the person she wanted to be.

He also didn't think less of her because she wanted to be rich, and never made her feel bad about how unwealthy she currently was.

"Morning, Nikki," Liam said on a sunny Sunday, both of them lying in bed side-by-side after Liam had slept over.

"Morning," she replied sheepishly, no longer scared of what Liam would think about her bare and sleepy face. He had seen her without makeup so many times now, and he loved her just the same.

"You know, I've been thinking about something…"

"What's that?" Nikki asked.

"Well… You know, considering how you work from home, and how we've been trying to spend more and more time together, but distance seems to be keeping us apart…"

"Yes?" Nikki felt her eyes lining with tears, her smile pulling at her cheeks.

"Would you like to move in with me? You and Scotty, that is," he offered.

Nikki felt her heart burst into a million happy pieces as she threw her arms around Liam and hugged him as hard as she could.

"Yes, yes, yes!" she yelped against his neck.

Scotty jumped on the bed with them, curious about all the fumbling and mumbling, and Liam rubbed behind his ears with one hand as he hugged Nikki with the other arm.

"I think Yardley will be very happy about this, too."

Liam left that afternoon after having lunch together to return to his home, and Nikki promised that she'd start doing everything needed so she could move in with him as soon as possible.

A COUPLE OF DAYS LATER, Nikki was reflecting on her and Liam's relationship while she went over her socials and looked at all the amazing comments her followers had left on her last picture with Liam. In it, they were seen at a terrace in a nice restaurant, glasses of bubbles in both their hands as they celebrated the next step in their relationship.

Nikki hadn't told her followers that she was moving in with Liam yet, as she wanted it to be a surprise. Everything was moving very fast in their relationship, and Nikki thought moving at that kind of pace would've frightened her, but it didn't at all.

Liam made her feel like she was at home all the time. So, moving in with him simply made sense.

And it was in that moment, that realization dawning on her, when an email popped up on her screen.

Nikki dropped her phone at the name showing on her phone, both excitement and fear filling her petite body.

The email was from Nikki's favorite fashion company in New York. She had tagged them and messaged them so many times over the past few years, that getting something back from them felt like the biggest accomplishment in her life.

"Come on, Nikki, take a deep breath, and just look at it. You've got this, girl," she encouraged herself.

Scotty came to her, curling up by her feet as Nikki's hands trembled, and she opened the email.

Dearest Nikki,

We are writing to you today because your account has come to our attention. Your latest design has gotten so many views that it eventually reached our hiring board, too.

It's not often that emails like this one are sent out, but your talent and sense of fashion are undeniable. There's a program we're running at the moment for new interns, which could end up as a permanent position in our company. And we would like to formally invite you to be a part of it.

The information is attached to this email.

Please reply to it promptly as training starts by the end of this week.

It was signed by the **CEO** of the company herself, and Nikki's knees weakened so much that she ended up curled up on the floor alongside Scotty.

"Oh my god, Scotty, what do I do now?"

Scotty licked her cheek in response, and Nikki wondered what that answer might mean.

WHEN NIKKI CALLED Liam that night to tell him about the email, Liam was quiet for a moment before replying.

"If this is what you want to do with your career, then I think you should take the position. Even if it means you won't be able to move in with me."

"How long does it take to fall in love?" Every time someone asks that question, they get a different answer.

Because the truth is, the amount of time it takes is

relative. It may take a year for one person to fall in love, and five seconds for another. And all Nikki knew in that moment was that she finally understood her father's advice, and she knew that she had found someone who would be willing to put all of his effort into their relationship. Who would be willing to put her first.

CHAPTER 10

Nikki couldn't believe her luck. She was painting her nails pink on the porch in front of Liam's house, and the night was warm and peaceful. Both dogs were running around happily, the sun only gone a few minutes prior, and a soft glow was still lingering in the atmosphere.

Nikki and Liam had been living together for almost a year. Her relationship with him made Nikki understand why things hadn't worked out with Scotty, or any other guy she had previously dated, and the decision to move in with him had only taken her a split second. She'd written back to the fashion company thanking them for the opportunity, but she decided to let them know that it didn't align with her life at the moment.

Undeniably, Nikki and Liam were soulmates. He understood her completely, and they could communicate without words. Just staying at home, doing nothing with him, was better than any night out. There was a time when Nikki believed that happiness only existed in clubs and at the mall. How foolish she had been.

After her nails were dry, she took out her pink yoga mat and rolled it out onto the porch. The mat was a gift from a company she collaborated with often. She put the phone on her tripod and pressed record.

"Hi, guys! It's your girl, Nikki! Are you ready for our evening yoga class?"

Nikki was sure to channel Liam's energy. It was fate. And ever since that day, she started becoming more and more spiritual. She hadn't abandoned her career in influencing; of course not, and she also hadn't stopped designing clothes. Fashion was her passion.

But she started meditating, doing yoga, and posting spiritual quotes, too. Her social media had taken a huge shift, one that people had noticed, and more and better people had started following her.

People who were aligned with what Nikki wanted in life.

People loved the new Nikki, the one who lived by Lake Dogma with her gorgeous boyfriend, their dogs Scotty and Yardley, had an amazing fashion sense, did yoga, and even had her own yoga clothing line!

Yes, after thinking about it for a long time, and thanks to Liam's encouragement, Nikki finally started her own clothing line for comfortable, but stylish, yoga wear. She designed them all herself, and had a team of people working for her to make sure everything else happen.

Nikki's new jobs as both an entrepreneur and designer meant she could spend more time with her boyfriend, and he loved that much more than any job where she'd be away from him. On the odd occasion, Nikki still made dresses by request, and had even been brave enough to accept her first wedding dress proposal from a few weeks back. The design was only half-way done, but she worked on it every spare moment she had. The wedding was to take place at the hotel near Liam's house, and she had even been invited to it!

LATER THAT EVENING, while Nikki was live and teaching her yoga class, Liam crept up behind her with a violinist. Nikki looked through her legs from her downward dog position and almost fell on her head, her heart racing.

Was Liam…? No, it couldn't be, not while she was on camera! As the violinist began to play, Liam got down on one knee, and Nikki started to cry from her crumpled position on the ground. *He's proposing!*

The comments on her video were blowing up; they were witnessing Nikki's proposal in real-time, something no influencer had ever done before.

"My sweetest, Nikki, will you make me the happiest man on Earth and be my wife?" Liam asked as he presented her with the beautiful ring.

"Yes! A thousand times, yes!" Nikki cheered with excitement. And this time, there wasn't a shadow of a doubt in her mind.

He placed the giant diamond ring on her finger, and Nikki showed it to the camera. She waved at her followers and then turned the camera off, throwing her arms around Liam in an endless hug.

Some moments were meant to be enjoyed alone.

Nikki and Liam danced through the night to the music as the violinist continued to play, the stars twinkling above, and Scotty and Yardley curled up on the porch, watching the couple with their heads cocked to the side as if listening to the music, too. And right there and then, Nikki decided that she had never felt happier in her life.

"I WILL NOT TURN into a bridezilla. I will not turn into a bridezilla. I will not turn into a bridezilla," Nikki repeated into the mirror as she fixed her hair and makeup, waiting for her bridesmaids to show up. A bit of uncertainty was creeping up her back, making all the hairs on her body stand on end.

As happy as this day was for her, old traumas were resurfacing as memories of her failed wedding filled her mind. Nikki had also thought that the day she married Scotty would be the happiest day of her life, but no, this was different.

Liam accepted her as she was. He loved her. Cared for her. And she loved him. Cared for him. Was sure she wanted to marry him. It didn't take a wedding to set Nikki off; her stress threshold was much lower, and she knew how to deal with her emotions now. Liam had seen many outbursts in their early months together, and he was still here. He still cared. He still helped her get better and deal with her emotions in a way only he knew how to.

And somehow, through his acceptance, Nikki had become calmer.

"I will not turn into a bridezilla. I will not!" Nikki said one more time, just in case.

And then the answer came to her, very clearly. That was the power of affirmations!

Nikki sat down carefully, making sure not to ruin the dress, and she placed her phone on the tripod that was by the wall. Then she clicked *live*.

"Hey, guys! Your girl, Nikki, here. Most of you

have been with me since I was still single, and also with me through the Scotty drama. And now, you're with me through this. Liam is my soulmate; there's no denying that. But I can't help but feel anxious about this day. Old wounds are resurfacing, and bad memories have made their way to my core. We have ten minutes before my bridesmaids arrive, so I want you all to join me in a shared meditation during the time I have left. Let's create an aura of peace together. And for those new to meditation, to whom ten minutes seem like forever, you can just open your eyes and tell me if my makeup needs fixing in the comments!" Nikki laughed at the camera, and then closed her eyes.

It was true. A ten-minute live meditation was all Nikki needed. Some cynical person might have pointed out that meditation was the most intimate act, but it was something she had learned to share with others. She had learned to be open and vulnerable, and it changed her life. When Nikki opened her eyes again, she felt refreshed and much calmer.

And that's exactly when Demi knocked on the door.

"Are you ready?" she treaded carefully, still standing on the threshold.

"Completely," Nikki answered.

"Do you want me to fetch you some cigarettes?" she asked next.

"Oh, no. I haven't had one in almost a year," Nikki quickly said. "By the way, I never apologized for the way I treated you during the wedding with Scotty. I know it's been a long time, but this is bringing it all back, and I'm sorry, Demi. I was a real bridezilla." Nikki grabbed her friend's hand and squeezed it tightly as she ushered her inside the room.

"That means a lot, Nikki. But chin up. My wedding is coming soon, and I'm not sure I'll be any better!"

They both laughed and hugged each other, as it was true that Demi had a bit of a mood when she got nervous, too.

"Let's get you married now, shall we?" Demi asked when they broke off the hug. "The photographer is waiting for Liam's arrival. He wants to capture the moment perfectly. After that, we'll have a bridesmaids' photoshoot, and then we're headed for the ceremony. By the way, such a great idea to have the wedding in the yard; the view of the lake is gorgeous!"

They walked over to the porch that overlooked the yard, where Liam was standing with his back turned. Nikki walked down the steps and carefully moved over the grass toward him as the photographer took photos vicariously. When she was right behind him, she called out his name, tapping him on the shoulder gently.

And then he turned around.

Liam looked at her with teary eyes and smiled like a little kid, pure joy in all of his features. He took a hand to his chest, pulling his emotions in check for a moment before lifting Nikki off the ground and kissing her.

"I am the luckiest man in the world," he whispered into her ear.

And Nikki couldn't help but think that wasn't true, that she was even luckier than he was.

***

THE CEREMONY WAS short and sweet. Scotty, the yorkie, was wearing a black tie around his little neck, and Yardley had on a baby blue one. They both walked in before the bride, the crowd cheering at their entrance, and then they sat and looked at their owners happily, not understanding what was going on at all. And surely, not understanding why all these people had gathered in their backyard.

The same violinist from their proposal played instrumental songs from Nikki's favorite artist. Their families and friends were all there, Mia and Demi both as bridesmaids.

As Nikki walked down the grass aisle, she enjoyed the attention to the fullest. Even though this was her second wedding, it was her first walk down the aisle. Her heart was bursting in her chest as her father held her arms, and they walked toward the love of her life together. She felt like the star of her own show.

"You chose wisely," her father whispered in her ear before leaving her at the altar, where the minister started his speech.

It wasn't long before the waited words were said in front of them.

"Do you, Nikki, take this man to be your lawfully wedded husband, to have and to hold from this day forward, for better or for worse, for richer, for poorer, in sickness and in health, to love and to cherish, from this day forward until death do you part?"

"I do," she said without hesitation.

"And do you, Liam, take this woman to be your lawfully wedded wife, to have and to hold from this day forward, for better or for worse, for richer, for poorer, in sickness and in health, to love and to cherish, from this day forward until death do you part?"

"I do," he answered, staring into her eyes.

"You may now kiss the bride," the minister said.

And so, they did. They kissed like it was the first time, like it was the last, like it was forever, and the people surrounding them cheered and whistled like it was the happiest moment in their lives, too.

"So, this is what it feels like to love the moment of the picture you post," Nikki whispered to herself, pulling Liam in for another kiss as the crowd cheered louder.

The End

HOW **NOT** TO BECOME AN INFLUENCER

KATHRYN REIGN